Library of Congress Cataloging-in-Publication Data
Gingerbread man.
The gingerbread man / illustrated by Bonnie and Bill Rutherford.
p. cm.
Summary: A freshly baked gingerbread man escapes
when he is taken out of the oven and eludes
his pursuers until he meets a clever fox.
ISBN 0-307-10681-0 (alk. paper)
[1. Fairy tales. 2. Folklore.] I. Rutherford, Bonnie, ill.
II. Rutherford, Bill, ill. III. Title.
PZ8.G3976 2001 398.21—dc21 [E] 00-046255

The Gingerbread Man

illustrated by

Bonnie and Bill Rutherford

A Golden Book ✶ New York

Golden Books Publishing Company, Inc.
New York, New York 10106

ONCE long ago in a little old house lived a little old man and a little old woman.

The little old woman worked in the house all day, baking wonderful cakes and pies and cookies.

The little old man worked all day in the garden. In the evenings, he ate the wonderful cakes and pies and cookies that the little old woman had baked.

One day the little old woman said to herself, "What can I bake for a surprise? I am tired of the same old cakes and pies and cookies…. I know, I'll bake a gingerbread man!"

Carefully she cut out the gingerbread man. She used two lavender gumdrops for his eyes, a licorice drop for his nose, and a red candy heart for his mouth. She put peppermint-drop buttons on his jacket and made a hat of mint-green sugar. Oh, he was a lovely gingerbread man!

When she had placed him in the oven, she hummed a little song, thinking of how delighted the old man would be when he saw his surprise.

After a bit, the little old woman opened the oven door to see if the gingerbread man was done. *Swish!* Out he jumped, and ran right across the kitchen!

"Stop!" cried the little old woman. "You are to be a surprise! We want to eat you!"

But the gingerbread man laughed and said, "Run, run, as fast as you can, you can't catch me, I'm the

gingerbread man!" And he ran out the door and past the little old man in the garden.

Up jumped the little old man. "Stop! We want to eat you, gingerbread man!" he shouted as he ran after the little old woman who was chasing the gingerbread man.

But the gingerbread man just laughed. "Run, run,
as fast as you can, you can't catch me, I'm the gingerbread man!" And the little old man and the little old
woman soon became tired and gave up the chase.

The gingerbread man kept running down the lane.
Soon he saw a brown cow grazing in the shade.
The cow twitched her tail when she saw him.

"Stop, gingerbread man! I want to eat you!" the
cow mooed.

But the gingerbread man just laughed and ran faster. "Run, run, as fast as you can, you can't catch me, I'm the gingerbread man! I've run away from an old woman and an old man, and I can run from you, too, old cow, I can, I can!"

Soon the cow grew tired of running, but the
gingerbread man kept on.

After a while, he passed a large black horse rolling in a field. The horse looked surprised to see a runaway gingerbread man.

"Stop! I want to eat you!" he neighed.

But the gingerbread man just laughed and said,
"Run, run, as fast as you can, you can't catch me,
I'm the gingerbread man! I've run away from an old
woman and an old man, and from a cow, too, and
I can run away from you, I can, I can!"

And he soon left the horse far behind him.

By and by, he met a yellow cat sunning herself in a daisy patch. "Stop! I want to eat you!" the cat mewed hungrily.

But the gingerbread man just laughed and boasted, "Run, run, as fast as you can, you can't catch me, I'm the gingerbread man! I've run away from a little old woman and a little old man, a brown cow and a black horse, too, and I can easily run away from you! Yes, I can!"

The gingerbread man ran faster. The cat ran after him until she saw another daisy patch, and being very tired, she lay down in the sun again. Then, just ahead of him, the gingerbread man saw a river. A red fox was sitting on the bank, blinking in the sun.

"Hello, gingerbread man," said the red fox. "Are you going across the river? I've just finished a *huge* dinner and I'm about to swim back to my home on the other side. Would you like to ride on my back?"

The gingerbread man thought about it. Surely it would be all right, since the fox said he had just finished his dinner.

"I'll climb up on your tail," the gingerbread man said. *That should be safe enough*, he thought.

"Of course," agreed the fox. He jumped into the sparkling river. "It's getting a little deep now," he said. "Maybe you'd better climb onto my back—just to keep dry, of course."

The gingerbread man climbed onto the fox's back. *That should be safe enough*, he thought.

"Oh my, it's really deep now," said the fox as he swam along. "Maybe you'd better climb up on top of my head, gingerbread man!"

And so the gingerbread man did just that.

"Oops, be careful," said the fox. "I think you'd better climb onto my nose so you won't fall off!"

The gingerbread man reminded himself that the fox had just eaten a very large dinner. He climbed onto the fox's nose and—*POP!* That sly old fox gobbled the gingerbread man right up!

And that was the very last gingerbread man ever
to come down the lane, past the cow and the horse
and the cat and the fox. For the next time the little
old lady baked a gingerbread man, she was careful
to keep the oven door closed until the little old man
was all ready for his very special surprise.